Third Wing Publishing

Text and Illustration © 2016 Oksana Zbarsky
Written by O.J. Zbarsky
Illustrations by O. Nenazhivina

ISBN: 978-0-6927235-0-0

Library of Congress control number:
2016912532

Published by:
Third Wing Publishing, LLC
570 Hampton Road, Unit 8
Southampton, NY 11968
www.thirdwingpublishing.com
Zbarsky@thirdwingpublishing.com

Printed in China,
10 9 8 7 6 5 4 3 2 1

# Do You Know Where the Freckle Goes?

written by O.J. Zbarsky

illustrated by O. Nenazhivina

Once upon a time there lived a small brown Freckle.

The Freckle went from nose to nose
looking for a place to live.

She lived on the nose of a very nice lady.

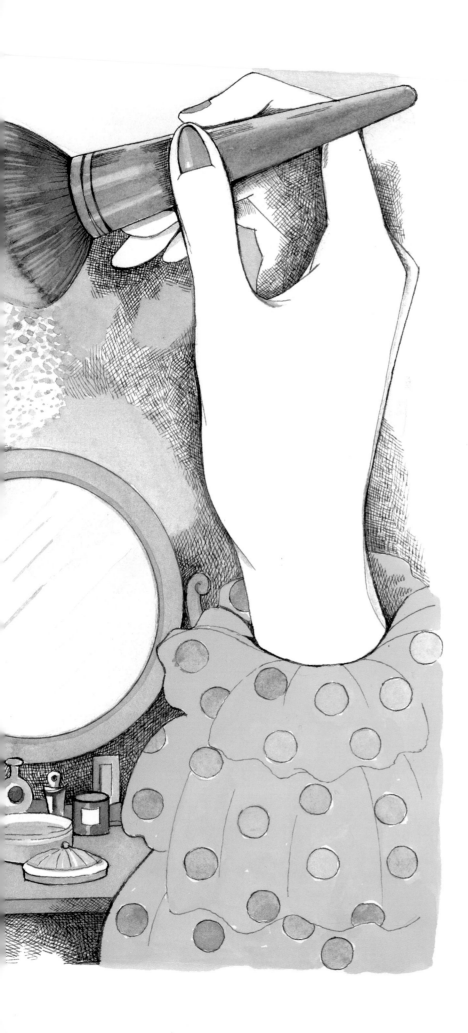

But the lady
did not like
the Freckle; she
would cover it
up with makeup.

The Freckle decided to move to the nose of a young man.

It was springtime, and the young man was always sneezing and coughing.

The Freckle
had no time
to rest.

One day, the Freckle moved to the cheek of a small girl. At the playground, she met a nice boy with a big smile on his face: Daniel.

The boy saw the little girl playing all by herself and decided to share his toys with her.

The Freckle
thought Daniel
was so nice and
handsome she
decided to move
to his nose.

She loved going to school with him.

She would
listen to all of the
interesting
stories the
teacher would
read to the class.

The Freckle and Daniel went to baseball games together, and the Freckle was so happy whenever Daniel hit a home run.

The Freckle
listened to
Daniel's scary
stories about
monsters.

And watched him as he made up fun games with his friends.

She was so happy living on Daniel's nose that she invited all of her Freckle friends.

Soon, Daniel's cheeks were covered in Freckles!